THE GAME NIGHT MURDERS

THEODORE HUNTINGTON

Dedicated to Laura.

"I'M GONNA CUT YOU!"

The party froze at Kerri-Anne's completely unprovoked threat. What was a fun Game Night at Linda's house immediately turned dark, with the dozen or so guests staring dumbfounded, jaws dropped, at the statuesque blonde, everyone wondering if this was a bad joke.

On cue, Alexa stopped playing the hip-hop party tunes that next-door neighbor Ren had requested. Ren was a regular at Linda's Game Nights, often the life of the party with his over-the-top perverted sense of humor.

After an uncomfortable ninety seconds of dead air, Linda's significant other, Gregory, finally replied, "What the fuck, Kerri-Anne?!"

Gregory stared down Kerri-Anne, noticing her glassy gaze and lack of balance while she struggled to remain atop the bar stool.

"You heard me," Kerri-Anne slurred as her shaky, freshly manicured index finger wiggled millimeters from Gregory's nose.

This was not the first time Kerri-Anne threatened Gregory, but it was the first time she let her feelings be known to the entire group. She had made constant remarks in private to Gregory, comments such as, "You're not gonna steal my best friend from me" or "You won't be around much longer". Gregory sluffed off those remarks as drunken banter from a jealous woman.

He and Linda had discussed Kerri-Anne's behavior many times, and Linda knew her friend was becoming a thorn in her relationship with Gregory. The couple speculated that Kerri-Anne was possibly a lesbian or bisexual, whose emotional connection with Linda had grown beyond that of "friend." The problem was, at least in Kerri-Anne's mind, Linda did not have the same intense feelings toward Kerri-Anne. In fact, after being single for over a decade since her twenty-year marriage ended, Linda had finally met a man with whom she felt a genuine connection. She could see spending their golden years together ... provided they could endure the bump in the road created by Kerri-Anne.

The other party guests could see the problem as well. They all walked on eggshells around Kerri-Anne's drunken antics and spoke frequently amongst each other about how Linda needed to cut ties with Kerri-Anne, who had sabotaged far too many Game Nights. There was the night Linda had to leave the party early to bail Kerri-Anne out of jail after she had assaulted an Uber driver because the Iranian immigrant would not play Kerri-Anne's favorite Sirius XM channel. And there was the night when Kerri-Anne had emerged from the bathroom completely nude, encouraging all the other partiers to join "enjoy the freedom of nudity". And when no one obliged, Kerri-Anne verbally assaulted the party guests, calling them "vanilla pussies" and "limp-dick Republicans". There were numerous other incidents of similar infamy, all which Kerri-Anne claimed to never remember after sleeping off her hangover.

Linda continuously assured Gregory that Kerri-

Anne would never really harm him. Gregory was not so certain.

Gregory noticed the twelve-inch carving knife within two feet of the inebriated forty-year-old woman's left hand, and not so subtly slid it away from her reach.

Linda emerged from the restroom, unaware of the strange interchange between her friend and her beau.

Kerri-Anne's demeanor changed immediately.

"What's with all this goop in your hair?" Kerri-Anne asked, stumbling to her feet to stand behind Ren, running her long fingers through Ren's thick black locks. She had played this flirtatious game with Ren for months. She had even confided in Linda about late-night booty calls at Ren's, none of which were true. It was all a smokescreen.

Ren held up a hand to block Kerri-Anne's. "Hey! I spent thirty minutes on the 'do tonight. Keep your grimy digits outta my fur."

Everyone laughed. Not Kerri-Anne.

"Oh Ren, you're such a freak. Why don't you go back to your murder spree?" Kerri-Anne sat back down on her bar stool, nearly missing the chair altogether. It was Gregory who caught her arm and saved Kerri-Anne from crashing to the floor.

The "murder spree" crack was another running joke among the Game Night crowd. Ren lived a mysterious life. He had no significant other, just a slew of unimportant hookups. Ren was a nuclear engineer who spent most weeks on the road, returning on weekends to his lovely mid-century modern home with a view of the Rocky Mountains. At one Game Night, someone jokingly asked if Ren was traveling the U.S. racking up serial kills. "Yup, and I bring them back and bury the bodies under my house," Ren replied. He enjoyed having an air of mystery around him and played into the banter.

Acting hurt by Ren's diss, Kerri-Anne left her bar stool and plopped down onto the living room couch, still within earshot of the other party guests. She whipped out her phone from her pocket.

"Hey, Hank! Why aren't you at the party? Where the fuck are you, Hank?" Kerri-Anne ended the voicemail message and tossed her phone onto the couch, unaware that it slid between the cushions. She always misplaced her phone; the Kerri-Anne iPhone search was typically the final activity of every Game Night.

"Let's go over to Hank's house. He's just around the corner," Kerri-Anne announced.

"No one's going over to Hank's house," Gregory spoke for the entire group.

"He never responded to the invite, Kerri-Anne. He never does anymore. What're you doing?" Linda asked.

"Come on, let's go!"

Kerri-Anne slipped on her denim jacket and opened the front door, looking back at the others. "Fine, I'm going to Hank's. Keep an eye on Chip for me." Chip was Kerri-Anne's Chihuahua, who always traveled with her.

No one was interested in going to Hank's, especially Gregory. Hank and Linda had dated briefly before Linda and Gregory met. The relationship ended amicably, and both Hank and Linda moved on with their lives. Linda kept Hank on the group text invite list just to be polite, but Hank never attended any more Game Nights. Kerri-Anne, however, was adept at driving wedges between people. Even after seven margaritas, Kerri-Anne could not stop her conniving jealousy. She brought up Hank every chance she could, knowing it was a sore subject with Gregory. Anything to drive a wedge between Linda and Gregory, she thought.

Game Night continued as the teams got back into Cards Against Humanity. But now the game could flow smoothly without Kerri-Anne's constant disruptions.

A cool breeze blew in from the front door, as Kerri-Anne stumbled back inside. She had been gone for all of five minutes.

"Shit, you're back already?" Ren quipped.

Flipping off Ren, Kerri-Anne grabbed Linda's arm and yanked her toward the back patio. "We need to talk."

The glass door slid shut, blocking the sound of Kerri-Anne and Linda's conversation from the rest of the guests. Gregory paid close attention to what was transpiring on the patio. He could not read lips, but it was evident there was a problem.

"I NEED TO TELL YOU SOMETHING," Linda whispered to Gregory while they slid under the covers. The party went well after Kerri-Anne had passed out on the couch, allowing the rest of the guests to enjoy the evening without her disruptions.

"Okay, what's up?" Gregory knew Linda was about to discuss Kerri-Anne, but he wanted to keep an even keel.

"Promise me you won't be mad."

"I don't know what you're going to tell me."

"Just promise, okay?"

"Alright."

Long pause. Linda was choking back her tears. "When Kerri-Anne dragged me out back ... she told me Hank is still in love with me."

"Uh-huh. Do you think that's true?"

"No, not at all. She's being ridiculous. Hank was *never* in love with me. In fact, I don't think she even went to Hank's. She was back here two minutes after she left."

"So, why would she tell you that?"

"I think we both know why."

Gregory waited for Linda to say it.

"It's so weird for me to admit this."

Gregory said nothing.

Linda took a deep breath. "Fine … she's in love with me. Are you happy? You were right all along."

THE "PURPLE RAIN" RINGTONE on Linda's iPhone sang for the sixth time. It was just six a.m. but the party had extended far later than she had expected, and Linda did not get to bed until after two a.m. So, Linda had stuffed plugs into her ears to help ensure at least seven hours of uninterrupted slumber. No such luck.

Linda cracked open an eye to see the time on her phone. While doing so she also noticed the slew of calls from Juanita, Hank's new bride. Neither Linda nor any of her friends from the party were aware that two weeks prior, Juanita's status changed from Hank's girlfriend to Hank's wife.

Juanita had never called Linda. Linda knew something was wrong.

"Hello?" Linda wiped the night goop from her mouth and cleared her throat.

Gregory too had hoped to sleep in much later. He'd heard the phone ring but tried to get back to sleep. Linda's conversation kept Gregory awake. He could clearly hear Juanita's end of the conversation, even though Linda did not put the phone on speaker, and she tried to keep her voice down.

"Linda, I'm so sorry to bother you this early."

"What's the matter, Juanita?"

"It's Hank. He went out last night to walk Mongo, but he never came home." Mongo was Hank's cherished ten-year-old bull mastiff.

"Oh no! What time was that?"

"Like … around three in the morning. Mongo was scratching at the door. I heard Hank get up. He kissed me on the forehead and said he'd be right back. I must've fallen back to sleep. And then I woke up to Mongo barking at the front door. He had on his harness and was dragging his leash, but there was no Hank."

"Where have you looked?"

"First, I went on the path where Hank takes Mongo over by Harvey Park. I called his name and looked for any clues." Juanita was a dispatcher for the Centennial, Colorado police department, so she tried to think like her detective coworkers. "When I came back home, I noticed Hank didn't take his phone. I looked at the history. He had three unanswered calls from Kerri-Anne at ten last night. And then a bizarre text from her. Let me read it to you …"

"Okay." Linda turned to see if Gregory was still awake and noticed he had slipped out of bed and was in the bathroom.

"She wrote, 'Why aren't you answering your phone, asshole?'"

"Sorry, Kerri-Anne was really drunk—"

"There's more. 'We need to talk. Linda is still in love with you. Meet me outside your house.'"

"Juanita … it's not true at all. I don't know—"

"Don't worry, Linda. I know. She's a fucking train wreck. Why do you think we stopped going to your Game Nights? He can't stand that woman. But I'm afraid—could she have done something to Hank?"

"That makes no sense, Juanita. Kerri-Anne has her issues, but she'd have no reason to be angry at Hank."

"Maybe she was waiting for him outside the house. Maybe they had an argument. It's possible, right?"

"Let's not jump to conclusions. Have you called the police?" Linda could not picture Kerri-Anne harming Hank. Hank was a big man—at least six feet and pushing three-hundred pounds. Kerri-Anne was five-seven and did not weigh more than one-thirty.

"Just a few minutes ago. They're sending a detective. I'm going to tell the detective about Kerri-Anne's text. I know she's your close friend, but she might know something."

"I understand., Juanita. Hank'll turn up soon. I'm sure he's fine."

Juanita's voice trembled. "I hope so. Will you let me know if you can think of anything?"

"Of course."

The toilet flushed and Gregory emerged from the bathroom.

"Did you hear?"

"Some of it. Hank's missing?"

"Juanita suspects Kerri-Anne."

Gregory shrugged his shoulders and wrinkled his face to convey, "Do you blame Juanita for thinking that?"

Linda's mind went through a mental timeline of events from ten p.m. until Kerri-Anne's Uber arrived at two a.m. Kerri-Anne remained asleep on Linda's living room couch until midnight when the first guests to leave, Linda's work friends Laureen and Maureen, bid adieu. Kerri-Anne did not get up, but she slurred, "Drive safe!" when the door closed behind Laureen and Maureen.

Linda encouraged Kerri-Anne to sleep in the guest bedroom. She told Kerri-Anne she could spend the night, but Kerri-Anne insisted she would go home once she sobered up. Linda recalled Kerri-Anne passing Gregory as she walked down the hallway to the guest bedroom, leaning into Gregory's ear to whisper, "You're a lucky mother-fucker, Greg." That was at one-thirty.

When Ren walked home at two a.m., Linda knocked on the guestroom door. Kerri-Anne was already awake, dressed, and getting Chip into his harness. Linda told Kerri-Anne an Uber was on the way. Kerri-Anne hugged Linda for an uncomfortably long time. Linda offered Kerri-Anne a cup of coffee while they waited for the Uber, which she declined.

Linda double-checked her Uber app and saw that Chike arrived at 2:08 a.m. to take Kerri-Anne home. Chike sent a thank-you for the twenty-percent tip at 2:29 a.m.

That gave Kerri-Anne thirty-one minutes to potentially make the fifteen-minute drive back to Hank's home. Kerri-Anne had taken an Uber to Linda's house, so her car was still in her garage, and by the time Kerri-Anne arrived at her apartment, she was sober enough to drive.

Linda worried that Juanita's concern was valid.

3

———

IT TOOK ALL OF KERRI-ANNE'S MIGHT to peel herself off her bathroom floor. She had spent the prior hour retching a horrid combination of fish tacos, green chili, and about a half-gallon of strawberry margaritas.

Kerri-Anne stuck her head under the bathroom sink faucet to rinse some of the skank out of her mouth. Then she limped her naked body five steps to her king-size bed, shoved most of the pillows to the floor, and plopped down on the brand-new comforter she had purchased with her severance check.

Chip scampered up the doggy steps to the bed and climbed atop Kerri-Anne-s chest, sniffing the vomit stench emanating from Kerri-Anne's mouth.

Kerri-Anne pushed her tiny dog down to her crotch, where Chip curled up and nestled into the warmth.

"You know you can't stay there all night, Chippers," Kerri-Anne said, fiddling with her Chihuahua's funny ears.

Chip looked up briefly at his human as if to say, "No, silly woman. I will be here as long as I desire."

"What the fuck is wrong with me, Chip?" Kerri-Anne's hand left the dog's head and squeezed the tears out of her eyes. "What does she see in Gregory anyway?" She emphasized *Gregory* in the most sarcastic tone possible. "He's not rich. He's okay looking for a guy pushing sixty. I give him a six-point-five. But Linda's a solid nine. She said he's good in bed, but that'll start fading soon. A guy his age is bound to lose the ole libido. And what's with his name, Chip? Gregory?! What a snob! How about just 'Greg' like every other Gregory on the planet? He's just not … shit, Chip … he's not … me!"

Kerri-Anne wiped the tear that rolled down her cheek.

Just before Kerri-Anne's eyes finally shut, she caught a glimpse of the clothes draped over the edge of her hamper. Her head tilted a bit to the side at the sight of a blood spot on the gold silk panties she had worn that night. She had hoped that Linda might get a chance to see Kerri-Anne's new lingerie collection—another purchase she had made with the severance check.

As she nodded off, Kerri-Anne mumbled, "How the fuck did blood get on my panties?"

4

IT TOOK EVERY OUNCE OF STRENGTH for Juanita to drag Mongo to the backyard. The police had finally arrived but would not enter the home with a two-hundred-pound canine protecting his home like a lioness guarding her cubs. Even after the massive canine retreated to the backyard, he continued to jump up on the six-foot wrought-iron fence, knocking loose one of the long metal poles.

"I'm sorry about Mongo. He's very sweet once he gets to know you," Juanita said, holding her screen door open for the two detectives. Mongo continued to bark for several minutes, each WOOF! rattling the back door.

"Coffee?" Juanita asked. "I just made a pot."

"Sure, I'd love some. Black, please," Detective Lauren Gabriel declared. Detective Gabriel looked more like a fashion model than a police officer. She came from one of those "long lines of law enforcement" families—Daddy was a cop, as was Grandpa, and Great-Grandpa as well.

Lauren was the only child of Raymond and Rae-Lynn Gabriel, so there were no sons to carry on the family tradition. Raymond Gabriel had taken a bullet in the back ten years prior from a petty thief who had stolen a carton of cigarettes. The bullet partially paralyzed Raymond and ended his career. It was the proudest day of Raymond's life when his daughter Lauren made detective at the tender age of twenty-eight.

"None for me," added Detective Ned Kranepool, whose doctor had recently ordered him to cut down drastically on caffeine, dairy, alcohol, and nicotine, or risk a heart attack within a year. A weather-beaten forty-year-old man in a terribly wrinkled brown suit, Kranepool could have passed for sixty. Kranepool was initially fuming when partnered with young upstart Lauren Gabriel. But over the two years since, he had grown to respect the woman, who had some of the most innate crime-solving skills he had seen in his fourteen years on the force.

The detectives sat next to each other on the black dander-filled couch. Juanita set the saucer down on the makeshift coffee table that Hank had hammered together using plywood and thick branches from the apple tree in their yard.

"I'm sorry about all the dog hair." Juanita noticed the fur attaching itself to Detective Gabriel's neatly pressed maroon suit. "Let me get a towel—"

"Please, ma'am, don't worry about it. I have three dogs myself," Gabriel explained. "Please … sit. And thank you for the coffee. Smells lovely." Detective Gabriel blew on the steam and slurped a sip. She smiled and tipped up the cup toward Juanita. The coffee was delicious and just what Gabriel needed so early in the morning.

Kranepool pulled an old-school notepad from his jacket while Gabriel set her iPhone on the table and pressed "voice record".

"Mrs. Sanguillen—"

"Juanita," she corrected the detective, spinning her new wedding ring as a reminder to herself that she had recently become "Mrs. Hank Sanguillen".

Detective Gabriel continued, "Juanita, we normally will wait at least twenty-four hours before initiating a missing person's report. But what was different in this case was the dog."

"Mongo?"

"Yes, Mongo showing up without his owner is a pretty unusual situation, especially at three a.m."

"We'd like to take a look at Mongo's leash and harness, if you don't mind," Kranepool requested.

"Of course." Juanita reached to grab the leash off the hook by the front door.

"Hang on!" Gabriel called out. "Better not handle that. There may be some evidence on it."

Detective Gabriel stood and walked over to examine the leash. "Hmm …"

"What is it?" Juanita asked.

"Not sure. Could be blood splatter. Could be mud. We better get forensics out here. You've already handled the leash, so whatever evidence might be there could already be tarnished."

"What about the dog, Detective Gabriel?" Kranepool asked.

"Good point, Ned. They'll have to examine Mongo as well."

Detective Gabriel continued her questioning. "I hate to ask this, and I'm sorry if it seems insensitive, but how were you and Hank getting along? Any arguments, problems between the two of you?" Gabriel sat back down on the fur-filled couch and gulped her coffee.

"No, I get it. I work for the Centennial P.D.—dispatch—so I know you have to ask. But things couldn't be better with me and Hank. We literally just got back from Maui—our honeymoon." Juanita flashed her sparkly new wedding ring.

"Oh, very nice," Lauren Gabriel replied. The beautiful detective had no desire to marry. In fact, she quite enjoyed playing the field, a frequent user of hook-up apps such as Tinder and OKCupid. None of her colleagues knew of her sex-positive lifestyle, although many of the single men in the department, and a couple of married ones as well, had tried to get to know her better, with no luck. Lauren would not shit where she ate.

Detective Kranepool, a two-time divorcee, could not help but roll his eyes at the sight of a new wedding ring. Kranepool had only recently paid off his second wedding ring, the one that wife number two threw at his eye following a nasty drunken fight.

"Thank you." Juanita was beaming, recalling her sex-filled honeymoon. Her smile faded quickly as her mind returned to the matter at hand: her husband's disappearance. "There is something that might help."

Juanita filled the detectives in on Kerri-Anne's texts and phone call.

"What do you know about this Kerri-Anne?" Kranepool prodded.

"Hank used to be friendly with her."

"Friendly?" Kranepool interjected.

"Not like that, Detective. He used to socialize with a group that would have regular Game Nights. They were usually at Linda O'Neill's house. She lives just around the corner. Hank stopped going to the parties after he and I began dating seriously. I only went to one party. It was fun, but kind of wild. Not exactly my crowd. The widest of the bunch was Kerri-Anne, Linda's BFF. I don't remember her last name. Harper ... Henderson ... something with an 'H'. Harmon! That's it, Harmon. Kerri-Anne is hardcore. She drinks a lot. I mean *a lot*. She thought she was the life of the party, but she was just a buffoon. And mean! She was just awful to Hank, always making fun of his weight. I think she had a problem with Hank because he and Linda dated. It was never serious, but Kerri-Anne acted all butt-hurt whenever Hank spent any time with Linda. It was like she had to control Linda's social life."

"Why was she trying to get Hank over to the party last night?" Gabriel asked.

"I have no idea. He hasn't been to a Game Night in like a year. Maybe longer. But Linda has a serious boyfriend now, so I think that has something to do with all this."

"How so?" asked Detective Kranepool as he noticed a pink piece of paper on the coffee table. He lifted the paper while listening to Juanita.

"I'm just speculating here, but if Kerri-Anne had such a tough time with Hank dating Linda, then she would likely lose her shit—pardon my French—over Linda and Gregory." Juanita refilled Lauren's coffee.

"Does this Greg guy have a last name?" Kranepool asked. He kept eyeing the coffee, which smelled heavenly. It was almost as difficult for Kranepool to give up caffeine as it was for liquor.

"Hmm … not sure. I've never met him."

Detective Gabriel reminded Juanita to visit the police station and fill out a missing person's report so Hank's disappearance could get entered into the system.

THE DETECTIVES SAT in their Crown Victoria, Gabriel behind the wheel, contemplating their next move. They had already contacted forensics to visit Juanita's house and dust Mongo and his leash for evidence. They wondered if Mongo would allow the forensics team to get close to him.

"So, pay a visit to Linda O'Neill or this whack-job Kerri-Anne?"

"O'Neill's around the corner, so that's stop number one," Detective Gabriel replied, noticing Kranepool's odd stare. "What? Something on my face?"

"You still smell like that coffee. You know I'm trying to—"

"Oh, get over it, Ned. It's good to have a little willpower." And with that, Lauren plunged her hand into a bag of Krispy Kreme donuts and gobbled one down in two bites.

"You got some sugar on your cheek ... bitch." Despite their twelve-year age difference, Kranepool and Gabriel had a fun rapport and enjoyed razzing each other.

5

KRANEPOOL PUSHED THE RING DOORBELL for the third time.

"I can hear something in there. Can you hear it?"

Detective Gabriel moved her right ear against the door. She raised an eyebrow. "They're fucking." Gabriel smirked. "I can hear the headboard banging and someone moaning."

Kranepool walked off the front stoop to the window, which he assumed was the master bedroom. He leaned his face toward the window.

"Ned! Stop being a perv. We'll come back later. Let's go find that Kerri-Anne woman."

"ARE THEY GONE?" Linda asked Gregory, who was watching the detectives drive away from a small gap in the bedroom blinds.

"Yeah, they're gone."

"I think we dented the wall," Linda said while examining the space between the headboard and the wall, where the couple had been ramming the oak bedframe while moaning phony cries of passion.

"Explain to me why we didn't want to talk with the

cops?" Gregory asked Linda, feeling the dent in the wall created by the headboard.

"They're gonna ask us all these questions that we're not ready to answer."

"Like?"

"Like … why did Kerri-Anne go to Hank's last night? And … what was Kerri-Anne's state of mind? I don't want to throw my friend to the wolves."

Gregory was listening to Linda, although he had wandered to the kitchen to brew the couple some coffee. He came back holding two steaming mugs.

"Thank you. I need this," Linda said, smelling the fresh brew before taking a small sip.

While looking at the damage to the wall, Gregory smirked. "Hey, since we already made this dent, we might as well shake the headboard again. This time without any clothes."

"Read the room, my witty porn star. I'm too stressed for sex right now."

"YA HEAR THAT?" Kranepool snickered to Detective Gabriel, his ear pressed to Kerri-Anne's front door. "This one's bumping uglies with someone too."

Lauren folded her arms and scoffed. "That ain't the sounds of passion, you perv."

"My ass it ain't," Kranepool replied. "Just listen to all that passion in there."

"She's barfing, you idiot. You should know that sound—intimately."

Detective Gabriel stepped in front of her partner and knocked loudly on the front door. Chip the Chihuahua went into full guard-dog mode, attempting to tear through the door with his tiny claws.

"Freaking Chihuahuas," Kranepool groaned over the dog's yapping. "Meanest sombitches on four legs. I'd rather deal with that monster mutt at Juanita's."

Detective Gabriel pounded her fist on the door five more times.

"Ma'am, we know you're in there! We can hear you retching!"

The door opened slowly, revealing a woman clutching a tiny dog. The woman had clearly seen better days. Her hair had specks of vomit dripping from it. Her eye makeup had smudged so much that she looked like she had gone three rounds with Mike Tyson.

Kranepool held up his badge. "Detectives Kranepool and Gabriel, Denver Metro PD. Can we have a word?"

"What's this about, Detectives?" Kerri-Anne blew out a belch that stunk like a sewer, forcing both detectives to take a step from the stench.

"Just a few minutes of your time, ma'am. If we can please come in?" Gabriel asked politely.

"Um, sure." Kerri-Anne escorted the police duo into her apartment, a two-bedroom that she usually kept tidy. "Excuse the mess," she added, while scooping piles of clothing from the couch, still holding Chip in one arm. "Have a seat, please."

Kerri-Anne dumped the clothes pile on top of the washing machine and returned to the living room. Chip began to squirm.

"Pardon me one sec. I'm gonna toss Chippers into the bedroom. He's not always friendly."

While waiting for Kerri-Anne to return, Kranepool and Gabriel scanned the apartment. They made mental notes of the numerous photos hanging on the walls and atop the mantle and breakfast bar of Kerri-Anne with another woman.

Kranepool stood and moved toward the breakfast bar for a closer look. When Kerri-Anne returned to the living room, adjusted her robe belt and settled into her tan recliner, Kranepool asked, "This your sister?"

"Huh?" Kerri-Anne asked, pulling her mangled hair into a ponytail.

"All these photos. The lady with you."

"Ahh, she's more like a sister than my real sister. Nah, that's my BFF."

"The BFF got a name?" Detective Gabriel probed.

"You know, not to be rude, but you still haven't told me why you're here."

"You're right, Miss … Harmon, right?"

"Yup. Kerri-Anne Harmon. Been my name all my life." Kerri-Anne's hangover had worn off, thanks to the stress of having two detectives sitting in her home.

"Do you know a Hank Sanguillen?" Kranepool asked. Then he tapped the photos of Kerri-Anne and Linda and sat back down in the living room.

"Sure, I know Hank. Why?"

"When was the last time you saw Mr. Sanguillen?" Gabriel asked.

"Um … I don't know. A few months ago … maybe more. Why? Is he okay?"

"Missing."

"Missing? What do you mean, missing?"

"Missing, as in no one knows his whereabouts," Kranepool elaborated. "His wife says he went to walk the dog at three a.m., and that's the last she saw of him."

"Whoa, whoa! Wife? Hank's not married."

"Oh, he's very much married. Saw the wedding ring, honeymoon photos, and the big wedding portrait on the wall. He's definitely married." Kranepool stared down Kerri-Anne. He knew she was lying and he wanted to gauge her reaction.

Kerri-Anne grabbed a lock of hair and started twisting it—a telltale signal of a fib.

"You were at Hank's house?"

"Yes, the home of Hank and Juanita Sanguillen," Detective Gabriel replied smugly. "She seems absolutely lovely."

"I, uh, I don't know her very well."

"That's funny," Lauren continued, "she knows you. How do you think we got your name?"

Kerri-Anne shrugged. The detectives waited for some sort of response. "Okay, but why would you think I have anything to do with Hank disappearing?"

Kranepool pulled out the notepad from his back pocket, flipping to the last page of notes. He read, "Why aren't you answering your phone, asshole? We need to talk. Linda is still in love with you. Meet me outside your house."

Kerri-Anne twirled her hair more vigorously. "What's that?"

Kranepool flipped his notepad closed and slid his pencil behind his ear, old-school style. "The text messages you sent to Mr. Sanguillen last night. Care to explain?"

"Fine! It's just banter. Hank and I are from New Jersey. We give each other a hard time. You know, like … 'the Giants suck; no, the Jets suck.' It's all good-natured."

"Ms. Harmon … there were also three phone calls you placed to Mr. Sanguillen at ten p.m. Sure seems like you wanted to get a hold of the man badly. This doesn't appear like good-natured banter, does it?" Detective Gabriel spotted a bead of sweat running down Kerri-Anne's temple.

"Detectives, I'm very sorry." Kerri-Anne took two deep breaths. "I'm feeling a bit under the wea—"

"Jesus Christ!" Detective Kranepool screamed and jumped back into his seat, feeling something crawling up his pant leg.

"I'm so sorry. That's Linny the iguana." Kerri-Anne pulled the reptile off the detective and placed it back into its terrarium. As soon as she clicked on the heat lamp, Kerri-Anne felt a surge of vomit race up her throat. She sprinted to the bathroom and heaved into the toilet.

"Fuck me," Detective Gabriel whispered to Kranepool. "This is a shit show. We're not getting anywhere with her in this condition. When she comes out, let's get her to come down to the station when she feels better."

"Why? For all we know, Sanguillen is fine. Maybe he's banging another woman and fell asleep at her place. Shit, he hasn't even been gone one day yet."

Gabriel nodded in agreement.

6

GREGORY WAS BALANCING perilously from the top rung of the ladder, digging his rubber glove covered arm into the rain gutter. He had promised Linda he would clean the gutters before she returned from her lunch date with Kerri-Anne.

A voice shouted out from across the neighbor's fence, "She's got you cleaning the gutters now?!"

Startled, Gregory turned quickly from atop the ladder, nearly losing his footing, a panicked look engulfing his face as he stared down at the twelve-foot drop to the ground. Gregory reached for the edge of the rain gutter, barely grasping on to regain his balance.

"Oh shit! I'm sorry, dude. Didn't mean to spook ya." Ren began walking toward Gregory, smirking at the sight of his friend scrambling to avoid a twelve-foot fall into the rose bushes.

Gregory ambled down from the ladder, tossing a clump of rotten leaves into the compost barrel.

"Better luck next time, huh?" Ren joked.

"What's that mean?"

"Ahh, never mind. Don't let me stop you from your honey-do chores."

"It's time for a break anyway," Gregory said, wiping the sweat from his brow, wondering if Ren was trying to scare him off the ladder. The guy did have a sick sense of humor.

Ren handed Gregory a cold Sam Adams. They clinked bottles and each took a refreshing swig. Gregory quickly forgot about the scare from the top rung.

"Fucked up about poor Hank, isn't it?"

"No shit!" Gregory escorted Ren toward the shaded patio in the backyard, where the two friends began speculating.

"I heard he was pretty messed up."

"Yeah, poor Juanita. She's not taking it well at all. She had to identify him."

"They're saying it was maybe a mountain lion attack."

"I hadn't heard that one," Gregory replied with a beer belch. "Mountain lion, huh? That doesn't make sense."

"Why not?"

"Mongo. I heard the dog was fine. If it was a mountain lion, Mongo would've had some damage too."

"Maybe," Ren replied. "Or maybe Mongo bolted. Hank was no sprinter. He couldn't outrun a lion."

Gregory shook his head. "Nah, that dog would have protected his human."

"What about the other theory?"

"You mean …?"

"I heard the cops have been questioning her."

The sound of Linda's Jeep Cherokee pulling into the driveway put a halt to the conversation.

"Linda and Kerri-Anne just got some sushi. Linda's trying to help Kerri-Anne get her mind off the Hank situation, so let's not—"

"No worries. Mum's the word." Ren made a clichéd key-lock motion on his lips.

"I see you're working hard on the gutters," Linda teased.

"Almost done. Ren came over with a beer, so I had to take a break."

"What's up, Ren?" Kerri-Anne slurred as the two hugged. Ren could smell the sake on Kerri-Anne-s breath. "You gonna help the old fart here with the rain gutters?"

"Fuck no! He's on his own there."

"I hope he doesn't injure himself climbing up that tall ladder," Kerri-Anne quipped, smirking at Gregory. "His bones are all brittle and shaky, ya know."

"Same old Kerri-Anne. You think maybe now isn't the best time to be a bitch?" Gregory retorted.

Kerri-Anne snapped. "What?! Are you gonna bring up Hank? No one was talking about Hank. Why are you stirring the pot, *Gregory*?"

"How 'bout I drive you home, Kerri-Anne?" Linda interjected. She turned to Gregory and mouthed, "Way too much sake."

"I HATE REN SO FUCKING MUCH!" Kerri-Anne blurted, staring out the passenger side window on the ride back to her apartment.

"What brought that on?" Linda asked, noticing Kerri-Anne's somber face reflected in her car window.

"He uses me. He used me at the party the other night."

"I don't understand. How did he use you at the party?"

"I told you. In the bathroom. The quickie?"

Linda was stunned. This was the first she had heard about a quickie that had allegedly taken place at Game Night. Stopped at a red light, Linda stared at her friend, but Kerri-Anne continued to peer out the window.

"I'm sorry. You and Ren had a quickie at my house that night?"

"The fucker was so high, he called me Linda while

he was banging me. Don't pretend you didn't notice. We knocked over a bunch of stuff off the bathroom shelf."

But Linda had not noticed. No one had noticed. In fact, Linda wondered if Kerri-Anne was possibly making up the entire story. After all, Kerri-Anne was sloshed, so drunk that she could have imagined the quickie, Linda thought.

Kerri-Anne had conjured an ongoing friends-with-benefits relationship between her and Ren. The fact was, the two only had sex once, a year ago, following a mushroom-filled evening when Kerri-Anne had followed Ren home from Game Night. The incident was so uneventful that Ren had completely forgotten about it. But Kerri-Anne's insecure mind could not accept the fact that Ren did not have romantic feelings for Kerri-Anne. So that one uneventful tryst turned into a steamy, secret relationship that only Kerri-Anne knew about. And now she was about to disclose everything to Linda.

"I've told you about me and Ren. We've talked about it several times."

"Umm, I think I'd remember that."

"Jeez, the guy is all over me at every Game Night. How do you not notice?"

Linda shook her head at that total lie. "Ren is all over—"

"Oh, come on! Everyone can see the sexual tension."

"Between *you* and Ren?"

The light turned green and Linda proceeded ahead, trying to focus on the road while listening to Kerri-Anne's farfetched tale.

"How long has this been happening?" Linda played along.

"Months. Maybe two years. Something like that. Nearly every Game Night, I sneak back to Ren's, and we bump uglies."

"But he's brought dates to Game Night several

times. There was Shelley … and Brenda—"

"A facade."

"They seemed real to me. Shelley really liked—"

Linda stopped short of arguing the point with Kerri-Anne. She was certain the relationship with Ren was a work of fiction, a smokescreen to pull the wool over Linda's eyes—an attempt to convince her friend that she was heterosexual. Linda did not want to burst Kerri-Anne's bubble. She was also a bit frightened. Kerri-Anne seemed committed to her lie. And she was. In fact, Kerri-Anne had convinced herself that she truly did have sex with Ren at the most recent Game Night and that Ren was the cause of the blood splatter on her panties. She was not sure how the blood transferred from Ren to the outer left cheek region of Kerri-Anne's undergarment. She was too drunk to recall if she and Ren had had a quickie in Linda's bathroom, but when one is blackout drunk, reality and fiction blur. Kerri-Anne knew her drinking was out of control. And she knew there were incidents that had occurred during her blackouts that she would not want to remember.

Kerri-Anne did not recall murdering Hank. But was it possible? Did a horrible rage come over the woman during her Game Night blackout?

Kerri-Anne would never know the truth behind the blood on her panties. But the truth was about as innocent as one might imagine. The truth was Kerri-Anne and Ren *did* have a quickie in the bathroom that night, unbeknownst to all the other guests. It marked the second uneventful sexual rendezvous between Kerri-Anne and Ren. An inebriated Kerri-Anne did not care if her sexual partners were male or female.

And the truth was Kerri-Anne also relieved herself in Linda's backyard while taking a cigarette break. While bending down, watering the rose bush in the dark, a thorn scraped her cheek. She was too drunk to feel the small cut. The blood was Kerri-Anne's after all.

7

DETECTIVES GABRIEL AND KRANEPOOL stared at the large monitor on what the detectives called the "crazy wall" where investigators attempted to construct crime details. On the monitor were images of Hank Sanguillen at the top of the pyramid, with photos of Kerri-Anne, Juanita, Mongo, and a mountain lion underneath, labeled "suspects". The bottom row of the pyramid was labeled "other party guests" with photos of Gregory, Linda, Ren, and several other Game Night guests.

"I know it sounds nuts," Ned started, "but I don't know if we should rule out suicide."

Lauren gave Kranepool the stink eye. "Yes, that's crazy."

"No, no, no. Hear me out," Kranepool continued. "He pretends to take Mongo for a walk, but leaves the dog in the driveway, or close to home, knowing eventually Juanita will see Mongo. And then Sanguillen walks to the river and offs himself."

"You saw the guy, right? Poor guy was mangled."

"True. Maybe a mountain lion or another animal got to him after he was dead."

"It's still crazy, Ned." Lauren shook her head.

"Why?"

"The guy just got married. You saw the big rock on

Juanita's hand. They had an amazing honeymoon. She was positively beaming. Why would the guy kill himself?"

"Maybe he did still have feelings for Linda. Maybe Kerri-Anne was right after all." Detective Kranepool pulled a pink piece of paper from his jacket pocket. "And maybe this is why he committed suicide." Ned smoothed out the sheet of paper onto the desk.

"What's that?" Detective Gabriel asked.

"Ahh, old Ned Kranepool did a little extra sleuthing." Ned looked proud of himself. "It's a termination notice. Picked it up from the Sanguillen home when we were questioning Juanita. Hank Sanguillen was laid off from his job at Xcel Energy. Seems Hank had an attendance problem, and electrical linemen aren't allowed to be high on the job."

Detective Gabriel picked up the pink slip to examine it. "It's dated September fifth. The day he died."

A STEADY RAIN FELL throughout Hank Sanguillen's funeral, but that did not deter nearly two-hundred mourners from paying tribute to the man cut down in his prime at age forty-three. It was a closed casket. The funeral director was not able to perform enough of his magic to make Hank's mangled body look somewhat normal.

The Game Night guests attended the funeral: Linda, Gregory, Ren, Laureen, Maureen, and Kerri-Anne. Many of Hank's former coworkers paid their respects. Hank came from a big family—seven brothers and sisters—who were all in attendance, as well as Hank's parents, Henry Sr., and Martha, who was nearly catatonic. Juanita sobbed throughout the entire ceremony. Hank's brother Ramone delivered an emotional, funny, and poignant eulogy.

Detectives Lauren Gabriel and Ned Kranepool sat in their Crown Victoria, carefully examining the attendees from their vantage point one hundred yards away.

"Look at her. She's not even paying attention to the eulogy," Detective Kranepool sneered while peering through binoculars.

"Let me see." Lauren yanked the binoculars away from her partner.

Kranepool was correct. Kerri-Anne was busy trying to flirt with Ren, whose body language made it clear that he wanted nothing to do with Kerri-Anne's antics. She was also clearly drunk.

"No fucking class!" Detective Gabriel snipped. "She has her hand on that guy's ass."

"That's Renaldo DeJesus," Kranepool clarified. "Linda's next-door neighbor. The guy Kerri-Anne is allegedly boinking."

"He's pissed. You should see his face. He wants nothing to do with Kerri-Anne."

Ren grabbed Kerri-Anne's wrist and removed it from his derriere. Then he switched seats with Gregory, which annoyed Kerri-Anne to no end. The angry glare she gave Gregory was priceless, but no one noticed, or maybe no one wanted to give Kerri-Anne any attention for being so disrespectful as Hank Sanguillen was laid to rest.

Linda decided to do something about her friend's behavior. She tried to remain inconspicuous but stood and walked behind Kerri-Anne, whispering something in her ear. Linda was no doubt chastising her inebriated friend for her outrageous antics. Kerri-Anne, attempting to apologize to Linda, twisted herself and leaned her chair backward to hug her friend. The chair leg slid in the mud, and Linda had to catch her friend from tumbling into the sludge. Despite a slew of nasty stares and "tsk-tsks" the funeral continued, uninterrupted by Kerri-Anne.

"Who goes to a funeral drunk out of their mind like that?" Ned asked rhetorically.

"Someone who feels guilty and wants to mask it."

"I still say—"

"I still disagree. The guy was murdered, and the murderer is right here under our noses." Detective Gabriel focused the binoculars as she zeroed in on something interesting. "Well, I'll be a motherfucker!"

"What?"

Lauren rolled down her driver side window and leaned out into the rain, focusing the binoculars even more.

"What is it? I can't see anything." Kranepool tried to lean over his partner's shoulder for a closer look.

"She put it away already."

"Put what away?"

"Linda O'Neill ... she just slid a pair of panties into Kerri'Anne's pocket."

"Are you sure? Panties?"

"Not a hundred percent sure. Hard to see through the rain. But it was definitely a small white garment, and she did not want anyone to see."

IT WAS WEDNESDAY. That meant something special for Kerri-Anne. It was her "Costco Day", the day when she and Linda would spend an inordinate amount of time and money strolling through the megastore, buying several items that were not on their lists.

Wednesday was also the day that Gregory had to work from his downtown office. He normally worked from home, but on Wednesday Kerri-Anne and Linda would have the house all to themselves until Gregory returned from work. Linda was able to juggle her therapy schedule so her Wednesday client list was light. She and Kerri-Anne would meet at Costco at 11:00 a.m., shop to their heart's content, grab a huge slice of Costco pizza, then adjourn to Linda's where they would overindulge on a couple of bottles of wine that they had just purchased.

It was Kerri-Anne's favorite day of the week. It was the one day when the unemployed human resources manager did not worry about her work status. She still had some money left over from her severance pay, and Linda often bought Kerri-Anne's Costco haul for her.

Linda and Kerri-Anne had just about drained their second bottle of Bodgea Garzon Tannat Reserve. It was time to let loose.

"Alexa," Kerri-Anne shouted, "play 1980s dance music!"

"Shuffling the one hundred greatest dance songs of the 1980s," Alexa replied as Whitney Houston's "I Wanna Dance with Somebody" began.

"Alexa, louder!" Kerri-Anne demanded.

Linda held up her wine glass. "To Hank."

Kerri-Anne did not reciprocate the toast to Hank. "You gonna ruin the mood?"

"C'mon, Kerri-Anne. I know you two had your issues, but let's pay our respects."

"Those cops think I killed him."

"They would have arrested you by now," Linda replied.

Kerri-Anne begrudgingly clinked their glasses. "Fine … to Hank."

Holding the remnants of the wine bottle high in the air, Kerri-Anne seductively shimmied around Linda, while Linda shook her considerable assets in Kerri-Anne's direction, both ladies singing along with Whitney.

Linda popped open a bottle of Kirkland Prosecco while Salt-N-Pepa's "Push It" played through the virtual personal assistant. By the time The Pointer Sisters' "I'm So Excited" began, Linda and Kerri-Anne were both shedding their clothes onto the floor. They were completely nude by the conclusion of Prince's "When Doves Cry".

GREGORY'S CAR LIGHTS BEAMED through Linda's bedroom window, startling the secret lovers, who sat up quickly in bed, both looking very much like they had spent the prior three hours in a raunchy orgy.

"Fuck, Gregory's home!"

Kerri-Anne raced around Linda's home, gathering

her clothes. She darted into the bathroom to pull herself together while Linda kicked her clothing under the bed and wrapped herself in her warmest robe.

The unmistakable aroma of liquor and sex filled the home. Gregory knew that smell.

10

DETECTIVES KRANEPOOL AND GABRIEL stood outside Kerri-Anne's apartment door. Kranepool glanced at his watch. "It's eight in the morning on a Sunday. Where would she be?"

"You hear that?" Detective Gabriel asked her partner.

"I don't hear anything."

"Exactly. We've been knocking and ringing the bell for five minutes, and there's no barking. Little Chip would be making all sorts of noise."

"Maybe she's walking the dog."

Detective Gabriel tried to look inside the window, but the blinds were closed.

Detective Kranepool glanced around the small patio. Where there had been a Hibachi grill, a dog bed, and a litany of dog toys, now there was nothing. The patio was completely cleaned out. "Hey, Lauren ... she's gone."

Detective Gabriel nodded in agreement.

The detectives convinced the superintendent to open Kerri-Anne's apartment, revealing a totally empty apartment.

"It looks empty," building superintendent Franz Cruz commented.

Kranepool rolled his eyes at the obvious observation.

"You say she didn't give notice?" Detective Gabriel probed.

"No, no notice."

"She wasn't evicted, was she?" Gabriel asked.

"No, I would know if she was evicted. Miss Harmon always pay rent on time. No complaints, except for barking dog."

"And you didn't notice a moving truck?" Kranepool asked.

"I work until seven yesterday. Maybe she move middle of night," Cruz speculated.

"We can ask some neighbors," Kranepool said to his partner.

"You still think Sanguillen was a suicide?" Detective Gabriel asked Kranepool, giving him her best "know-it-all" look.

"We better talk to those Game Night friends," Kranepool said. "They'll probably know more than Harmon's neighbors."

GREGORY AND LINDA COULD NOT AVOID the detectives any longer. Kranepool and Gabriel sat in the couple's living room as Linda stood over the Keurig, waiting for Kranepool's coffee to finish dripping.

"Thanks for meeting with us," Detective Gabriel said. "We've been trying to talk with you for a while. You're tough people to pin down."

Linda handed Detective Kranepool his black coffee.

"Thanks." Ned set the cup on the coffee table. "Smells good."

"Whole Foods, 'Autumn Eggnog' flavor," Linda replied.

Ned took a sip and gave the java his thumbs-up.

"Horrible thing about Hank Sanguillen," Gregory said, stating the obvious.

"That's not really the reason for our visit," Detective Gabriel replied.

Linda and Gregory both looked confused.

"Kerri-Anne Harmon ..." Detective Gabriel began, "any idea where she is?"

Linda looked confused. "I'm not sure what you mean."

"Vanished," Kranepool said.

"Vanished?" Linda was more confused.

"Her apartment's been cleaned out. Empty," Kranepool continued. "Didn't even give notice. No forwarding address registered at the post office."

"That can't be," Linda said. "I just saw her a couple of days ago. We went to Costco. She never said anything about moving."

Gregory gave Linda a curious glance. The couple had not discussed the goings-on between Linda and Kerri-Anne, but Gregory wondered if Linda might know more than what she was letting on about Kerri-Anne's disappearance.

The detectives were suspicious as well.

"Seems pretty odd she wouldn't say anything to you." Detective Gabriel was staring directly at Linda.

"Me? Why me?"

"Come now, we know you two are close," Gabriel said, sounding angrier.

Gregory gave Linda another knowing glance, which Linda did not notice.

"Look, I have no clue where Kerri-Anne is. She even RSVP'd to my group text invite for Game Night tonight."

"Mind if we take a gander at that group chat?" Kranepool asked.

Linda hesitated for a moment, but then grabbed her phone from the kitchen counter, scrolled to the group chat, and handed the smartphone to the detective.

Lauren Gabriel held back the urge to click around

Linda's phone for additional text chats, especially those between Linda and Kerri-Anne. But she knew she would have to get permission to access those secret text chats. Detective Gabriel read through the group banter about Game Night, which included a long string of sad memories about Hank Sanguillen, as well as some funny memes and witty remarks. There was nothing incriminating, and nothing to indicate that Linda had any knowledge that Kerri-Anne would skip town.

"I'm going to ask, although I probably know your answer … but… any chance I can see your one-on-one chats with Kerri-Anne?" Detective Gabriel figured it was a long shot, but worth asking.

"I'm telling you, Detective Gabriel, you won't find anything in my phone—or anywhere—about Kerri-Anne moving."

"I can get a warrant for the phone records."

Detective Kranepool slurped his coffee, his eyes darting back and forth between Linda and Gregory, trying to gauge their body language and facial expressions.

"What's there to hide, hon?" Gregory interjected, eliciting a nasty glare from his significant other. But Gregory was a smart man. He figured the detectives might see some flirtatious comments between Linda and Kerri-Anne, but little else. And Gregory thought it best to eliminate any unnecessary suspicions the detectives might have regarding Linda.

Linda did not agree with her man. "I guess you'll just have to get a warrant, Detective. And take my word for it—I have no idea where Kerri-Anne went."

11

LIEUTENANT PIPPA CANNONE entered the war room carrying a pink box of Krispy Kreme donuts. She set the goodies on the table and flipped the lid open, teasing Detective Kranepool, who had been steadfastly sticking to his diet.

"You're a twat!" Kranepool barked, refusing to even turn around to see the donuts.

Detective Gabriel, on the other hand, had no qualms about snatching three sugary treats, stuffing one whole donut into her mouth before she sat back down.

"Thanks, Lieutenant!" Lauren mumbled, crumbs of donuts spilling from her mouth.

"Ya know, Gabriel, some of the boys around here think you're actually hot. They have no idea what a pig you are," Kranepool teased his partner, who smiled wide at Ned, donut remnants oozing from her perfect teeth.

"Alright, what do we have here?" Lieutenant Cannone got comfortable, staring at the images of the various players in the Sanguillen murder mystery.

Pippa Cannone was a Sicilian emigrant whose family relocated to the U.S. when she was a teenager. She still spoke with a slight Italian accent. The petite, raven-haired fifty-two-year-old divorcee was admired by all who served under her for the past decade since elevated to the lieutenant post. She was a brutally honest leader who had innate crime-solving instincts.

Kranepool explained, while aiming a laser pointer at the wall. "We have one Henry 'Hank' Sanguillen, deceased. His new bride Juanita reported him missing after Sanguillen took their mammoth dog Mongo for a walk at three a.m. and never returned."

"Is the wife a suspect?"

"Negative," Gabriel replied. "Newlyweds, very much in love."

"Alright, continue ..."

"We have the Game Night clan, led by one Kerri-Anne Harmon."

"She's the one who's gone AWOL?"

"Vanished like a fart in the wind," Detective Kranepool quipped.

"Making her the primary suspect?"

"Maybe. There's also Linda O'Neill, Game Night host, Harmon's BFF, and, according to the text messages we just got back, O'Neill and Harmon are more like friends with benefits."

"Sanguillen looks like a large man. How could either of these slight women have overpowered that guy?"

"Could have been both. We're not ruling out an accomplice," Detective Gabriel noted.

"What about motive?"

"Jealousy. Love triangle. All connecting to Linda O'Neill. Seems like all the suspects and the victims have or had some romantic connection with O'Neill," Kranepool added.

"So then, why would O'Neill be a suspect? Everyone loves Linda, right?"

"Maybe an argument went awry," Detective Gabriel replied. "Maybe Sanguillen was about to spill the beans to Linda's new boyfriend. It's a long shot, but we can't rule her out."

"Any other theories?"

Lauren Gabriel looked toward her partner. "Ned has some theories," she said with a raised eyebrow.

"Yes, Lieutenant. My skeptical partner disagrees, but Sanguillen had just been fired from his job. And even though he was a newlywed, his texts indicate he still had feelings for O'Neill. So—"

"Suicide?" Lieutenant Cannone speculated.

"Precisely."

"But no note or any other proof it could have been suicide," Gabriel added. "Cause of death was a deep puncture wound to the chest, which could have been caused by any number of things—maybe a fireplace poker—"

"And," Kranepool interrupted, "maybe a mountain lion claw."

"Another Ned Kranepool theory, I presume."

"He was found in the woods near the Platte River. Lots of wild animals wander those grounds in the middle of the night. And he was severely mangled. Clearly, some animals, ya know, did some damage to the poor guy."

"That most likely happened post-mortem," Gabriel noted.

"Hmm ..." Lieutenant Cannone pondered.

"What is it?" Detective Kranepool asked.

"Who's the guy to O'Neill's right?"

"Gregory Page. O'Neill's live-in S.O."

"Hmm ..." Pippa repeated herself.

"What is it, Lieutenant?"

"Everyone loves Linda. And the guy who's supposedly her main squeeze isn't a primary suspect?"

"Well, I have to admit," Detective Gabriel said, "he's flown under our radar."

"Have you checked him out at all?"

Silence.

"I'd say it's time to do a little digging on Gregory Page."

12

"HOW MANY TIMES DO I HAVE TO SAY IT?" Linda snapped at Gregory. "I'm not in love with her. We had a very minor fling. That was all. It was just a couple of times."

"I believe you," Gregory replied as he stirred the taco meat in the pan. "What bothers me more than anything is the dishonesty. I feel humiliated. I feel like a fool. What other secrets are you hiding?"

"I knew you'd react like this. That's why I never told you. It was meaningless to me."

"It wasn't meaningless to Kerri-Anne."

Linda had no reply.

"And it isn't meaningless to me."

"I know. I'm sorry. I didn't mean to hurt you. Or Kerri-Anne."

"Who else knows?"

"Why would we have told anyone else? Kerri-Anne knows this was a secret."

"Because Kerri-Anne Harmon gets drunk and babbles her bullshit to anyone. There's no way she can keep anything a secret."

Linda knew Gregory was right.

"So, while we're sitting around playing Cards Against Humanity, everyone else in the room is thinking what a buffoon I am … Linda's idiot, clueless boyfriend."

"Should we cancel Game Night?" Linda looked at the time on her iPhone. "It's already five, but—"

"No, we have all this food."

"I'll make this up to you, I promise." Linda's eyes welled.

"I have to ask you something else."

"What?"

"Do you know where Kerri-Anne went?"

Linda shook her head. "My hand to God, I have no idea."

THE GAME NIGHT GUESTS were engrossed in a new game, Pictionary Air, a fun twist on Pictionary, where the drawings, created with a Bluetooth pen, appeared on the television screen. Ren came up with a new rule: for each team's turn, they could make one of the other three teams drink the number of shots corresponding to the words they guessed correctly that round.

"Peacock!" Laureen yelled.

Maureen shook her head "no".

"Black cock!" Ren guessed.

"Jesus, Ren, are you always a pig?" Maureen snapped.

"Time's up!" Gregory announced. "That's two correct."

"Gregory, Linda, and Jesse"—a new Game Night invitee, a teacher at Linda's school—"drink!" Maureen grabbed the Patrón and poured three shots.

"To Hank!" Gregory, Linda, and Jesse clinked glasses.

Every shot throughout the evening was toasted in Hank's honor.

Up next were three female friends of Ren: Judy, Karen, and Yanika. All three were new to Game Night, and all three were already feeling the effects of the psychedelic mushrooms before the evening even began.

It was a strange Game Night. What was supposed to be a tribute to Hank—even though the man had not appeared at a Game Night for at least a year—had an uncomfortable cloud floating in the air. Linda and Gregory were tense over the revelation about Linda and Kerri-Anne. Kerri-Anne's absence was glaring, with constant whispers among some guests speculating about her whereabouts. And, of course, there was Hank's death. Juanita was invited to Game Night, and Linda called her several times, insisting it would help her to get out, have some fun, and toast Hank's memory. But Juanita stayed home, still deeply mourning her husband's death.

Ren's three "plus-ones"—Judy, Karen, and Yanika—added some comic relief. Ren had introduced the ladies as "just friends" but it was clear they were each competing for Ren's attention. Linda's coworker, Jesse, had been making some moves on beautiful African-American Yanika, who was not reciprocating at all. After five rounds of Pictionary Air, Ren's three friends had yet to score one point, although they were chosen for several rounds of tequila shots.

"I have another new rule," Ren suggested. "If you don't want to do shots, you can remove an article of clothing. Strip Pictionary!"

"No!" Gregory immediately reacted.

"Oh, come on, man! Lighten up," Ren replied.

"Are we getting naked?" asked the inebriated redhead, Judy, while removing her tight sweater. Then she sat on Linda's lap, wrapped her arms around Linda, and tried to kiss her neck. Everyone loved Linda.

"No! Ren, make them stop," Gregory said, tossing a blanket over Judy's shoulders.

And Game Night got significantly more uncomfortable.

Ren enjoyed the highly charged atmosphere. He had unsuccessfully attempted at several prior Game Nights to initiate more sexual adventure. He had grown tired of the "in memory of Hank Sanguillen" toasts. Ren also enjoyed making Gregory uncomfortable. He was friendly enough with Linda's man. But he was far more interested in Linda.

GAME NIGHT WAS WINDING DOWN. Ren had gotten his three lady friends each an Uber, shoveling their nearly comatose bodies into the cars. Jesse left soon after that, frustrated that his advances toward Yanika went unanswered. Laureen and Maureen had a smoke on the back patio before saying their goodbyes. Gregory flinched and wrinkled his nose as Laureen gave him a hug. The stench of Marlboros made Gregory nauseous.

Gregory stood over the sink, cleaning up the many dishes and the taco mess.

Ren poured himself another tequila shot. "To Hank!" he said sarcastically, tossing back the shot.

Linda was wiped. It was one in the morning and Ren was once again overstaying his welcome. Linda did not even say goodnight as she slid into the bedroom and shut the door.

"Alexa, play 'Ass and Titties' by Three 6 Mafia," Ren demanded.

Alexa began playing the raunchy hip-hop song.

"Alexa, stop!" Gregory yelled. "Read the room, Ren. Linda's gone to bed. It's just us two chickens left."

Ren did not get the hint. Instead of gathering his coat and walking home next door, Ren poured himself another shot.

"You seemed overly tense tonight," Ren said, stating the obvious.

"Lots of shit swirling around lately."

"Like what?" Ren was not that dense. He was playing dumb.

"Seriously? Hank's death ... Kerri-Anne disappears ... Game Night nearly becomes a drunken orgy ... "

"Are you really that uptight? We're all adults. You can't handle some naughty fun? Linda's parties were once totally wild."

"Wild? *How* wild?"

"Let's just say nudity was *not* discouraged." Ren knew he was getting under Gregory's skin. He was stretching the truth quite a bit. There was never any nudity or sexual antics at the Game Nights prior to Gregory's arrival in Linda's life. Ren just wanted to see how Gregory would react. He was drunk, still tripping on mushrooms, and in an obnoxious mood.

Gregory was not amused. The revelation about Kerri-Anne and Linda was still a fresh wound.

"Time to go, Ren."

"Oh, come on. Just one more drink. Have a drink with me."

"No, I'm tired."

"Fine, I'll have another," Ren said, pouring himself a tequila shot. "Ahh!"

"You happy now? Time to go." Gregory opened the front door.

Ren did not budge from the bar stool. "Tell me, Gregory. Did *you* do it?"

"Do what?"

"Come on, you can tell me. It's just us two here. Hank. Kerri-Anne. You did it, right? Both of them. Ya know ... get rid of the competition?"

"What the fuck are you talking about?"

"I can't figure out how. Did you wait for Linda to pass out? I know she wears earplugs to bed. I bet she didn't hear you get out of bed and go to Hank's house. But Kerri-Anne. Now, that's a mystery. How'd you get rid of her? Cleaning out her apartment. Stashing her car somewhere. That had to take some planning."

"You're tripping, dude."

"I've given this a lot of thought. I mean, it was easy to make Kerri-Anne the suspect in Hank's murder. Jeez, she was so drunk at that Game Night, she wouldn't even remember if she really killed the guy."

"Shut the fuck up, Ren!"

"You knew about Kerri-Anne and Linda, right? I'm sure someone had to have told you about Linda and Hank. That poor sap. He was so in love with Linda. I'm surprised he didn't try to whack you. Man, he was jealous when you started seeing Linda."

"You're fucking with me. Hank had just gotten married. He and Juanita were in love with each other."

Ren shrugged. His body language said, "Juanita was Hank's second choice."

Gregory pointed toward the open front door. He was fuming.

"Fine, fine, I'll go."

Gregory slammed the door behind Ren, nearly hitting him in the ass.

Good thing Linda wore earplugs to bed.

13

THE VIEWHOUSE NEAR COORS FIELD was once one of Detective Gabriel's favorite watering holes. There was a time when she and Detective Kranepool would frequently pour back a few IPAs there following a long shift. But since Kranepool's sobriety, Detective Gabriel had not been back very often. Instead, she would stop into The Cruise Room, The Upstairs Circus in LoDo, and other taverns where she could avoid detection by fellow police officers and find easy prey to satisfy her urges.

Lauren Gabriel had a high hit rate on Tinder. Every time she would swipe right, the fellow would reply promptly, eager to connect with the stunning law enforcement officer. She would meet first at a bar, and if she felt some electricity sparking, would insist that the man of the moment find an expensive hotel room for the rest of the evening.

For old times' sake, Ned Kranepool convinced his partner to join him at The Viewhouse for some bar snacks and to discuss the perplexing Hank Sanguillen/Kerri-Anne Harmon case.

"What'd you come up with on Gregory Page?" Lauren asked Ned, slugging back a Cosmopolitan.

Pablo, the tall preppy-looking waiter, adorned in a

52

Rockies' jersey and Broncos' ski cap, placed a plate of Southwest Chicken Quesadillas and Beef Sliders in front of Lauren and Ned, who shoveled an entire slider into his mouth in one bite.

"Squeaky fucking clean. The poster boy for the Boy Scouts." Ned slurped his Coke from a paper straw to wash down the slider.

"What's his story?"

"Fifty-two years old. Works from home. He's a marketing manager for an energy company. Been there for six years. Divorced, three grown kids. Moved into O'Neill's five months ago. No traffic violations. No arrests. Got his text messages. Nothing incriminating at all. Doesn't even send Linda any dick pics."

"Did that disappoint you?"

"No doubt. I've been itching to see his man meat," Kranepool joked. "And get this. He doesn't even have Kerri-Anne Harmon or Hank Sanguillen in his contacts. This guy's not connected enough to these people. I think we can cross him off our list of suspects."

"Maybe not entirely. But now what? Our primary suspect vanishes. No trace of her car. No one even saw a moving truck at her apartment. She hasn't used her credit cards. Is she dead? Is she running from us? Hiding in Brazil? What. The. Fuck?!"

"We need to get some warrants," Kranepool added. "Time to search for a murder weapon."

"Let's just hope that didn't disappear along with Kerri-Anne Harmon," Lauren replied. "And while we're at it, we should get a warrant for cellphone records from everyone else at that Game Night party. We need to cover all our bases. Something isn't adding up."

The bar crowd erupted as the big-screen TVs displayed a Broncos' touchdown.

"Weren't you dating that Broncos' wide receiver?"

Kranepool asked Gabriel, turning his attention to the game.

"It was one date, and that was a year ago."

"What was wrong with him? He made lots of money. Six-foot-two black dude. Probably had a gi-normous—"

"Don't go there, Kranepool!" Lauren held up her hand to Kranepool's face to change the direction of their chat. "Honestly, he seemed like a nice guy. We went back to his place. He was building a fire, and then he got all temperamental. The fire wasn't starting. He kept poking at the logs and losing his temper. It scared me a bit, a big guy swinging a ..." Detective Gabriel's voice tailed off.

"What? What is it?" Detective Kranepool asked, stuffing another slider into his face. He could make out the imaginary light bulb over his partner's head.

14

LINDA WAS WORKING LATE. She had several meetings with parents scheduled at her school. Gregory was home, finishing up his work, wondering what to prepare for dinner when Linda texted him:

Linda: Got invited to happy hour with a couple of teachers. Will grab some dinner at the bar.

Gregory replied to one more work email, then shut off his laptop for the evening. It was only four-twenty, but it was not worth it to begin a new project at that time of the day.

Standing in front of the open refrigerator for several minutes, Gregory finally decided to throw together some shrimp tacos when he received another text:

Ren: Yo, Gregorious! What'cha doing?

Gregory: Just about to make some tacos.

Ren: Linda home yet?

Gregory: She's working late.

Ren: Made some beef bourguignon. It's delish. Come on over. Call it a peace offering. I was a dick the other night.

Gregory: Well, yes, you were. A big, hairy, smelly dick. Beef bourguignon sounds yummy. What time?

Ren: Whenever.

. . .

DETECTIVES LAUREN GABRIEL AND NED KRANEPOOL were usually very thorough. But for some reason, they had been sloppy investigating Hank Sanguillen's death. First, they spent too much time debating various theories. Was Hank's death a suicide? Was he mauled by a mountain lion? Then they spent too much time focusing on Kerri-Anne Harmon as the primary suspect. And when Kerri-Anne disappeared, they spent too much time searching for her whereabouts. They had not looked at other potential suspects. They had not even searched for a murder weapon—something that the coroner's report noted was a "long, sharp, possibly metallic object".

Now that Kerri-Anne had disappeared, the likelihood of Ned and Lauren finding anything resembling a long, sharp object near her apartment was extremely remote. But she had to look.

Ned drew first dumpster duty. Rubber coverings over his hands and shoes, Ned rummaged through the closest dumpster to Kerri-Anne's unit, gagging on the odor of old eggs, diapers, and miscellaneous other trash. Lauren sat in the Crown Victoria, swiping left and right on her phone. She was careful to make sure Ned was unaware of her extracurricular activities.

"Found something!" Detective Kranepool stood up, hoisting a splintered baseball bat in the air.

Detective Gabriel shoved her phone into her jacket pocket and walked over to her partner. "What's that?"

"Louisville Slugger. Or at least the bottom half of one."

"Lemme see."

Kranepool held the broken bat out in front of Gabriel's face as the detective looked closely at the sharp end.

"Hmm ... no sign of any blood. I don't know baseball. Do wooden bats break very often?"

"Actually yes. They break all the time. If you hit the

ball on the label, or tight on the fists, they tend to shatter." Ned had played some ball during his college days at Colorado State, although he'd almost always swung an aluminum bat.

"We can bag it, and have it tested, but chances are pretty slim—"

Before Gabriel could finish her sentence, Kranepool tossed the busted bat back into the dumpster. "Let's keep looking."

The detectives scoured several other dumpsters at Kerri-Anne's apartment complex. They elicited the help of numerous uniformed officers to search the woods nearby, as well as the area near where Hank Sanguillen's body was found. Nothing resembling a long, sharp, possible murder weapon was found.

Next step: obtain search warrants for Linda and Gregory's home and Juanita Sanguillen's home.

Juanita was taken aback when the detectives appeared at her door with a search warrant. She was still deeply in mourning over her husband's death and angered by the possibility that her husband's murder weapon might be somewhere on her property.

Kranepool and Gabriel poked around the entire home, including the attic, the grimy dark crawlspace underneath the house, the garage, and the backyard. The closest thing to a murder weapon they could find was a set of golf clubs in the garage, which looked untouched. Hank Sanguillen had received the clubs as a wedding gift from his brother, even though Hank had never played—and never would play—a hole in his life.

Over at Linda and Gregory's house, the detectives caught Gregory just as he was leaving for Ren's. They flashed the search warrant at Gregory.

"Search all you want," Gregory insisted. "What're you looking for, anyway? A murder weapon?"

"Exactly," Kranepool replied. "You don't happen to have any long sharp objects stashed around here?"

"Search all you want," Gregory retorted. "Got nothing to hide here." Gregory held the door open for the detectives. "Just don't make a mess, okay?"

The detectives checked around as much of the property as they could. They opened the crawlspace and sifted through the boxes stored underneath the house. All the homes in the neighborhood had the same cramped little crawlspaces instead of basements. Ned Kranepool shrieked at the sight of a raccoon skeleton near the furnace, but he did not see anything suspicious.

The door to the garage was unlocked, so the detectives looked around there as well. The garage was stuffed with an abundance of holiday decorations—Linda was an avid Christmas collector—but there was nothing closely resembling a device that could have been used to kill someone.

Drake's song "Laugh Now Cry Later" sang out from Detective Gabriel's iPhone.

"Yes, Lieutenant?"

"Anything?"

"Fucking waste of time. All day searching for shit. How 'bout the marsh near Platte River? Anything?"

"A bunch of muddy shoes is all. Oh, and someone's lost dog was returned home. So, at least there was that."

"We're not gonna find a murder weapon, Lieutenant Cannone. It's probably buried along with Kerri-Anne Harmon."

"Go home and get some rest, Detective. It's been a long day."

"That it has," Lauren replied. "I'm exhausted and filthy—and I need to get cleaned up for a date."

"Oh, to be young and desirable. Well, have a good night, Detective Gabriel. Get back at it again in the morning."

Kranepool overhead the conversation. "Another date, Lauren? That's like three this week."

"Didn't know you were counting, *Dad!*" It was her fourth "date" but Lauren did not want to correct her partner.

LAUREN GABRIEL WAS PREPPING FOR HER HOOK-UP. She had on her favorite red pumps, black faux leather pants, and a low-cut pink sweater top. She squirted some Black Opium toward her cleavage and poured herself a glass of chardonnay. Looking at her phone, Lauren realized she still had thirty minutes before she was supposed to meet her date at the trendy RiNo-area (River North Art District) restaurant, Barcelona.

Lauren Gabriel knew she was living a dangerous dual life—a serious, decorated police detective and promiscuous, serial Tinder dater. She knew she had to slow down her secret, uninhibited side before something unscrupulous could happen. As a law enforcement officer, Lauren Gabriel knew damn well the potential dangers of her casual dating with unvetted individuals.

But Lauren Gabriel was addicted to the thrill. She tapped open her phone almost unknowingly. It had become an involuntary impulse.

Lauren scrolled and swiped. Left swipe. Left. Left, Left.

"Hmm, he's cute." Right swipe.

The next image looked familiar. Lauren paused. Renaldo D., forty-five, into jazz music, mid-century modern architecture, mountain biking, and cooking.

"I know this guy," Detective Gabriel said, drumming her bright pink manicured nails (the right index fingernail was chipped courtesy of the day's dumpster searches) on the arm of her couch.

"Holy shit! How did I not see this?" Lauren was so mad at herself for not realizing that she had dated Ren DeJesus, one of the infamous Game Night attendees.

She had stared at his photo on the wall at least two hundred times over the prior month. He looked slightly different than he did that night when Lauren met Ren at Linger for a drink. His hair in the Tinder profile was a lighter brown and he sported round, gold-rimmed glasses at the time. Ren now wore black glasses, and his hair was jet black. But it was unmistakably the same weirdo that freaked out Lauren two years prior.

Ren DeJesus was a perfect gentleman while at Linger. He ordered spicy pork potstickers, Korean fried chicken, and two sangrias. Lauren liked how Ren took charge. She was attracted to Ren. They discussed movies, wine, and books. Ren made not-so-subtle crude jokes and disclosed his "embarrassing" penchant for sex toys. After they polished off their food and three sangrias, Lauren suggested they get a room. Ren knew where to go. He texted Lauren the address to the Magnolia Hotel, a swanky place in downtown Denver with fireplaces in the rooms. Lauren followed Ren, sticking close behind Ren's GMC Hummer pickup truck. Lauren took a liking to Ren's confidence, his money, and his bad-boy image.

Lauren and Ren were nude within five minutes of checking into the hotel. Ren started a fire and uncorked a bottle of wine from the wet bar.

The gas fireplace did not need much work at all. It was odd that there was even a fireplace hearth set of tools—brush, tongs, shovel, and poker. Ren held the poker into the fire, pretending to move the fake logs around to stoke the flames. He rolled the poker around for an inordinate amount of time.

Lauren inquired, "What the fuck are you doing with the fire? Come over here and poke me instead."

And he did. Ren held the red-hot poker toward Lauren's nipple.

"Stop!"

"I thought you liked it kinky," Ren said, continuing

to aim the poker closer to Lauren's breast. She flinched, but Ren lunged forward and scorched the detective.

Lauren reacted quickly, kicking Ren in the balls and slamming his nose with the palm of her hand. His nose bleeding and groin reeling in pain, Lauren gathered her clothes quickly and ran out of the hotel room.

Lauren Gabriel had dated so many men in the interim that she'd nearly forgotten that traumatic evening. But now it all washed back to her.

"Motherfucker! Ren DeJesus! Why didn't I see it?

15

GREGORY AND REN WERE ENJOYING THEIR MEAL. Ren was an excellent chef. The two chatted mostly about music. They were kindred spirits when it came to their tastes in classic rock and music history. Ren's Onkyo Home Theater System blasted an ear-splitting one hundred fifty decibels and Gregory had to scream for Ren to turn it down every ten minutes. Ren was an avid IPA connoisseur and shared several bottles of Juicy Bits Double Dry-Hopped beer from Weldworks Brewing Company.

For most of the evening, Gregory nearly forgot about the issues weighing on his mind.

"Name the band," Ren challenged Gregory, tapping his iPhone paired with his stereo. Ren slid the volume up to ten as Roxy Music's 1975 song "Love is the Drug" blasted out of the speakers.

"Roxy Music!" Gregory replied a few seconds later.

Ren gave a thumbs up.

"But I can hear it just fine at like half the volume!"

Ren relented again. Gregory's ears were ringing.

Ren's Boston Terrier, Beaver, leaped into Gregory's lap.

"Beaver likes you," Ren noted as the elderly pooch stuck his snout into Gregory's beer glass.

Beaver hopped off Gregory's lap and darted out the little doggy door, allowing cold air to sweep into the room. It was an unseasonably cool November evening.

Beaver began barking, setting off a bark-a-thon with a chain of nearby dogs. One particularly boisterous beast-like bark nearly drowned out all the others.

"God-damn Mongo! That dog's part grizzly bear."

"Mongo?" Gregory asked.

"Yeah, Hank's dog. Well, he *was* Hank's dog."

"I didn't know Hank lived right behind you."

"Catty corner, but yeah. He was right back there." Ren pointed in the direction of Hank and Juanita Sanguillen's home.

Beaver darted back inside, shivering from the cold.

"I think it's gonna snow," Gregory predicted.

"Yeah, it's fucking cold. I'll start a fire. Beaver loves to curl up next to the fireplace." Ren tossed several logs into the inglenook, crumpled up some pages from an *Architectural Digest*, and lit the paper to start the fire. He grabbed the fireplace shovel and moved the wood around, stoking the flame.

Gregory could not help but notice Ren's fireplace tool set was missing an important piece. "What happened to your—"

Gregory did not finish his question. His mind instantly flashed to Detective Kranepool's question about "long, sharp objects." A chill shot down Gregory's spine. He froze in place, not wanting to look toward Ren.

Ren nonchalantly walked to the kitchen. "Let me get you another cold one. I have this other IPA called In the Deep Steep. You'll love it. Creamy and citrusy." Ren was back in the den a minute later, holding the beer out to Gregory, who reluctantly took it.

"Cheers!" Ren clinked bottles with Gregory, then he grabbed his phone and entered a new song. "Bet you don't know this one."

An obscure 2004 song by The Killers, "Jenny Was a Friend of Mine", blared. The lyrics were eerily appropriate:

> *Tell me what you want to know*
> *Oh come on, oh come on, oh come on*
> *There ain't no motive for this crime*
> *Jenny was a friend of mine*
> *So come on, oh come on, oh come on*
> *I know my rights, I've been here all day and it's time*
> *For me to go, so let me know if it's alright*
> *I just can't take this, I swear I told you the truth*
> *She couldn't scream while I held her close*
> *I swore I'd never let her go*

Gregory took a couple of large swigs, then sat down in the ultra-comfortable Hailee cowhide armchair, sinking deep into the leather.

"That chair's pretty fucking comfy, isn't it? Found it at a garage sale in Glenwood Springs for twenty dollars. How's the beer?"

Gregory took another gulp. "It's ... good." His vision began to blur. Gregory's mind raced. He shook his head to clear his brain. Gregory had to get out of Ren's house very soon. But how?

Linda had returned from happy hour with her work friends and settled down to watch *Firefly Lane* on Netflix. She poured herself a glass of Prosecco. Linda had no reason to worry about Gregory, who had texted her earlier that he was going to have dinner at Ren's.

A BURLY, MIDDLE-AGED MAN pushed open the squeaky back door of a church rectory. There were six people seated in a circle in the dining room. It was ten o'clock. Snow had started to fall, and the man tracked wet footprints across the floor.

"Welcome, friend," the chairperson said to Ned Kranepool, who felt the need to find a meeting that night. He had a lot on his mind. "Have a seat."

Ned squeezed in between an emo-looking young woman, who did not appear old enough to legally drink, and a weathered man with long gray hair who could have been the lead singer of a 1970s rock band.

"We were just doing introductions," the AA chairperson, Trixie, said to Ned in her calmest, soothing voice. "Care to share? I'm Trixie, by the way."

Ned smiled at Trixie. "Uh, sure," Ned began, as he peeled off his new winter coat, a recent purchase from Costco. "Hi, my name is Ned, and I am an alcoholic. Fifteen months sober." Ned held up his most recent coin.

"Hi Ned," the group replied.

"Congratulations on that, Ned," Trixie added. "You're new to our group."

Ned nodded.

"What brings you here at this late hour?"

"Well, I'm doing okay. Personally. You know, it's always a struggle. I have a rough day, and I want to drink. But I've been good. Strong. I lost my wife and my kids. Wrecked my car. I still have my job and ya know, it's a tough job. I'm a cop. But it's all I have, and I need it.

"It's the job that brings me here tonight. My partner, to be exact. She's a great detective. One of the best I've ever seen. And she's an addict. She thinks I don't know, but I know."

"Does she use on the job?" Trixie asked.

"Her addiction isn't drugs. It's sex. She's putting herself in danger. A lot. I see her on those apps all the time. I've followed her a few times at night. I'm, I don't know, I'm ... protective. She's young and beautiful, and ... and she's going to get hurt. I've seen it too many times."

"You need to stop her!" The emo-looking young woman stood and pointed an angry finger at Ned.

"Jovanna, please," Trixie said, "take a seat and let Ned finish."

Jovanna sat but continued, "No, I'm serious, dude. That was me like six months ago. Those apps are addicting. I was hooking up with like four or five guys a night. I'd bang one at his place, and then sometimes I was back on Tinder while he was still doing me, looking for the next one. It's no joke. Of course, I was high as fuck all the time, too. But I couldn't stop the sex … until. Well, until one sick fuck nearly threw me out his twelfth-story window because I wouldn't stay and fuck him again."

Ned knew outing Lauren and her sex addiction could potentially impact her job. He also knew Jovanna was right. Ned could not let Lauren continue to endanger herself. He had to be a good partner—and a good friend.

16

"CALL KRANEPOOL!" Detective Gabriel shouted to her Bluetooth, desperately trying to get a hold of her partner as she raced to Ren DeJesus' house. But the calls kept going straight to voicemail. Ned had turned off his phone while attending the AA meeting. "Where the fuck are you, Ned!?"

Traffic on I25 slowed to a crawl. The light snow that had begun to fall did not deter drivers from exceeding the speed limit and one reckless motorist lost control of his 1998 Subaru Outback, slamming into the guardrail and flipping onto the side. The accident stalled traffic for two miles. Detective Gabriel slapped her red-and-blue LED police light atop her Crown Victoria and maneuvered to the shoulder to skirt past the traffic.

Lauren tried voice texting Ned for the fifth time: "Kranepool—exclamation point—it's Ren DeJesus--period—I figured it out. No time to explain—period. On my way to his house now." Detective Gabriel was certain that Gregory's life was in danger.

Still no reply from Kranepool.

Detective Gabriel did not want to enter a dangerous home with a suspected murderer alone. She called it into the precinct, requesting backup at DeJesus' home.

She also called her lieutenant from the car:

"What makes you so certain it's DeJesus?" Lieutenant Cannone asked.

"I know the guy. It was a while ago, so it took some time before I recognized him. But I, uh, I met him. He was strange. Into sadistic stuff."

"Sadistic stuff? Like devil-worshipping?"

"No, like masochistic things."

"But you ran a check on the guy, right? He's one of those Game Night friends. Didn't he come up clean?"

Traffic came to a halt on the Federal Blvd. exit ramp. Detective Gabriel turned on her siren to get around the cars, but she was wedged in, bumper-to-bumper.

"Fuck me!"

"What's wrong?"

"God-damn traffic! I can't get around these cars." Lauren inched her car around the line of traffic at the clover leaf exit. "Lieutenant, I think Gregory Page is in danger," she said, scraping her front left bumper slightly against the steel guardrail. "Gregory was heading over to DeJesus' house when Ned and I saw him earlier this evening."

"What's the motive, Detective Gabriel? Why would DeJesus want to kill Hank Sanguillen, Gregory Page, and possibly Kerri-Anne Harmon? What would turn this guy into a serial killer?"

"Simple, Lieutenant. Love. The guy's in love with Linda O'Neill."

"What is it about that woman? Is everyone in love with Linda O'Neill?"

"YOU PUT SOMETHING IN MY DRINK," Gregory slurred.

"I put beer in your drink. That's all." Ren smirked at Gregory. "Not my fault you're a lightweight."

Gregory could handle a few beers. He could not, however, handle the LSD that Ren dropped into his beer. Ren thought it would be amusing to see how the usually buttoned-up Gregory Page would react to an unexpected acid trip. Ren had a sadistic side.

"You're going to kill me, aren't you?"

"Kill you? Why would I want to kill you?"

"Same reason you killed Kerri-Anne, and Hank."

"Now, you're just being paranoid. That's just the L —" Ren stopped short of admitting to dosing Gregory's beer.

"The detectives said Hank's murder weapon was a long, sharp, metallic object. Your fireplace poker. It's missing. You used it to kill Hank, didn't you?"

Ren glanced over to the fireplace, flames flickering. It was mesmerizing, especially for someone tripping on LSD.

"I suppose it is missing. That's inconvenient."

"You tried to kill me when I was on the ladder that day, didn't you? You wanted me to fall off the ladder."

"Gregory, Gregory, Gregory … you're having a bad trip."

Gregory wanted to leave, but he knew Ren would easily overpower him in his altered state. Gregory wobbled to his feet, his brain telling him to "Run!" But he could only make it a couple of steps before falling onto the orange-and-blue throw rug covered with geometric shapes that began to spin before Gregory's distorted eyes.

Ren let out a callous laugh. "Oh, man, no experience with lysergic acid diethylamide?" Ren finally admitted to dosing Gregory's beer.

Gregory curled up into a ball on the throw rug. He began to cry. "You put acid in my drink? Why? Just kill me now. Put me out of my misery."

Ren sat down on the bone-colored Joybird sofa. He picked up Beaver and set him on his lap, petting the dog and contemplating his next move. "What shall I do with poor Gregory, Beaver? He's so fucked up. What shall I do?"

Beaver let out a meek whimper, worried about the hapless neighbor writhing on the floor.

DETECTIVE LAUREN GABRIEL made a slow left turn onto Osceola Street, the Crown Victoria fishtailing slightly on the slippery new snow. Her backup had not yet arrived, so the detective pulled over to the curb, two houses in front of Ren's. She turned off the engine and took a deep breath, awaiting the arrival of the blue-and-white Ford Expedition cruisers.

Lauren checked her phone again for any response from her partner, Detective Ned Kranepool, who unbeknownst to Lauren, was attending a late-night Alcoholics Anonymous meeting, ironically looking for advice on how to help save his partner from her demons.

"Where the fuck are you, Ned?" the young detective pondered, worried her partner might have fallen off the wagon and holed up at some seedy bar.

The first cruiser pulled up behind Lauren's Crown Vic. Two tall African-American uniformed officers walked toward Detective Gabriel's car.

A group of dog walkers walked their Siberian Huskies across the street, slowing their pace, curious about the police activity on the normally quiet street.

"Officers," Detective Gabriel said, acknowledging the two men.

"Detective," Officer Aaron Guernsey replied with a slight grin. He was one of the numerous Denver policemen who had been pursuing the beautiful Lauren Gabriel. The two had met for a drink about a year prior, although nothing more happened.

Lauren Gabriel was committed to only hooking up with men outside the law enforcement community.

Officer Guernsey's partner, Sergeant T.J. Hamilton, caught his partner's wry smile, but he chose to ignore it. "What do we have here?" Sergeant Hamilton asked.

"Male suspect, Renaldo DeJesus, mid-forties, probably armed. He could have a potential victim with him inside. Next-door neighbor, Gregory Page.

"This the Sanguillen case?" Guernsey asked.

"Yup."

Another cruiser arrived with two more uniformed officers.

The police officers unholstered and drew their weapons as they approached Ren DeJesus' front door.

BOOM! BOOM! BOOM!

Eminem's "Stan", a song about a murderous fan, blared through the door.

"Renaldo DeJesus! Denver Police Department!" Detective Gabriel yelled, the four uniformed cops surrounding her.

REN HEARD THE BANGING on his door. He leaned down to Gregory, who was shaking in fear and curled in the fetal position on the floor.

Ren leaned his face down toward Gregory's. "You called the cops on me? What the fuck is wrong with you?"

Ren spun around in a circle, calculating his options. Ren's acid trip had just taken a nasty turn for the worse. He looked at Gregory, who had tears rolling down his cheeks. He looked at Beaver, who was unaffected by the situation, licking his butt.

"Want to switch places, Beav?"

BANG! BANG! BANG!

Officer Hamilton took off to cover the back of the house. But Ren had already left, sprinting out his sliding glass door through his backyard and scaling the five-foot fence. Officer Hamilton spotted DeJesus just as he was ascending the fence.

"He's on the run!" Officer Hamilton yelled into the lavalier on his sleeve. Hamilton took off after DeJesus but was immediately greeted by Beaver, who took great offense to a cop invading his territory and bit into Hamilton's leg. "Fuck!" Officer Hamilton shook off the small dog, but Ren was already a good one hundred yards ahead by the time he climbed the fence, blood running down Sergeant Hamilton's calf, courtesy of Beaver's fangs.

With the gash stinging his leg, Hamilton knew he would not be able to catch Ren on foot, so he grabbed his partner, and the two got back into their squad car to search for DeJesus.

Detective Gabriel entered DeJesus' home through the back entrance, spotting Gregory Page on the floor. He was not moving. The detective reached her hand out to Gregory's throat to check for a pulse.

THE TWO BLUE-AND-WHITES slowly scoured the neighborhood in search of Ren DeJesus. Several additional squad cars arrived on the scene, cordoning off a ten-block radius to through traffic, and quickly ushering residents and dog walkers back to their homes. Curious onlookers peeked through their windows to get a glimpse of the thrilling chase taking place in their suburban neighborhood.

Sergeant Hamilton spotted one overly curious elderly lady opening her front door, stepping onto her front stoop. The woman yelled toward the police cars, "You boys chasing down those drug deJelers!?! Too many of them potheads invading—"

"Get inside, ma'am! And lock the doors behind you!" Hamilton announced through his bullhorn.

The officers were moving in the wrong direction.

Ren had managed to climb on top of a nearby rooftop. He had an excellent vantage point where he could see most of the police cars traversing the area in search of him.

But Ren chose the wrong rooftop to hide. He chose a home where the very large dog could stand on his hind feet and spot a man crouching down atop the roof. He chose a home where the dog recognized him and wanted to get the man's attention.

"WOOF! WOOF!"

"Mongo, quiet," pleaded Ren quietly.

"WOOF! WOOF!"

"Fucking dog," Ren mumbled, lowering himself into Juanita Sanguillen's backyard, where he was immediately greeted by the massive hound.

Juanita Sanguillen watched with prying interest through her kitchen window.

Ren was able to free his leg from the humping pooch. He scaled the fence and fled in the opposite direction from where the police were searching.

DeJesus thought he was in the clear, sprinting toward Evans Avenue. He did not spot any police cars and could not hear any sirens or bullhorns. He slowed his pace and started toward The Green Solution dispensary, one of the numerous local cannabis establishments, and a place where Ren believed he could avoid the police search. His acid trip was in full bloom and Ren felt being among other like-minded people might calm his racing, frantic brain.

Ren reached for the door to enter the dispensary.

WHAM!

Ren DeJesus was tackled down to the cement. The two men rolled and tussled for a moment until the man's fist collided with DeJesus' jaw. He spun Ren around and slapped the cuffs onto Ren's wrists.

"Renaldo DeJesus," the man said, catching his breath, "you're under arrest for the murder of Hank

Sanguillen. You have the right to remain silent. Anything you say can and will be held against you. Do you understand these rights?"

"Yes, Detective Kranepool. I understand. How did you find me?"

"Mongo. I heard him barking at you, saw you jump off the roof, and followed you here. Dog's got an unmistakable bark. He's a good dog."

17

EPILOGUE

KERRI-ANNE HARMON was alive and well, staying at SOBA, a drug-and-alcohol rehab facility in New Jersey. Her parents had insisted that Kerri-Anne enter rehab, offering to pay for the treatment as well as a new home in the Garden State immediately following her release. Kerri-Anne had disclosed to her parents that she was the target of a murder investigation and that she could not recall any details of the night in question. Marvin Harmon, a seventy-year-old retired pastor, had had enough of his daughter's risky lifestyle. Kerri-Anne put up a meager fight, but she knew her parents were right. She needed help.

Kerri-Anne had called Ren to help pack up her belongings, and Ren arrived at midnight with his pickup truck, spending much of the night driving four loads of Kerri-Anne's possessions to a storage facility, also paid for by Kerri-Anne's parents. She did not want to contact Linda, knowing the goodbye would be too painful.

There were no records of Kerri-Anne's financial transactions, since they were all handled by Marvin Harmon, and her cell phone was confiscated and shut down while in rehab, so no one could trace her whereabouts.

. . .

REN DEJESUS was innocent of murder. But the missing fireplace poker, scores of lewd text messages to Linda O'Neill, and his escape attempt when the cops arrived amounted to substantial circumstantial evidence against Ren. DeJesus could not explain why he ran, except that he was under the influence of LSD. It did not help his case when Detective Lauren Gabriel testified before the Grand Jury about her date gone awry where DeJesus tried to scald her breast with a fireplace tool.

One year to the day after Hank Sanguillen was killed, Ren DeJesus was sentenced to twenty years in prison for manslaughter.

Ren's dog, Beaver, would go live with Gregory and Linda, who took excellent care of him.

GREGORY PAGE survived the acid trip and life-threatening events at Ren's house. His life, in fact, was never in danger. Ren had no desire to murder Gregory, although he did harbor a burning desire to re-kindle his affair with Linda.

Gregory insisted Linda pull the plug on her Game Nights. And although Linda had gotten such pleasure from her parties, she knew there were too many ghosts swirling around the events.

Gregory's new passion became being a pet owner. He and Beaver clicked. The two would hike together every weekend. Gregory would even get a companion for Beaver, another Boston Terrier he dubbed "Richard".

LINDA O'NEILL came clean to Gregory about her numerous flings, including Kerri-Anne, Ren, and Hank. She worked through her sex addiction, thanks to weekly sessions with a very skilled therapist, Dr. Victor Greenberg, a man with nearly fifty years of experience as a psychoanalyst.

Gregory applauded Linda's turnaround, although he secretly wondered if Dr. Greenberg had fallen in love with Linda. After all, *everyone* loved Linda.

LAUREN GABRIEL also sought help with her addiction, although she was not successful. Lauren attended regular Sex Addicts Anonymous meetings at the same church rectory as Ned Kranepool's AA meetings. But there were too many temptations. Men were constantly hounding her. Tinder proved to be the tip of the iceberg. She found numerous other ways to meet men online.

Detective Gabriel's careless lifestyle would prove her undoing. The shining star of the Denver Police Department was shot in the back by a crazed eighteen-year-old who Lauren first met on Tinder and then, just ten minutes later, she was having sex with the young man in an alley behind Nocturn, a bar in the RINO district of Denver. She was paralyzed for life, just like her father. The man, blinded by the drug Ketamine, was enraged when Lauren would not go back to his home with him.

Lauren Gabriel worked a desk job for the rest of her career.

NED KRANEPOOL was not as fortunate as his partner. Ned remained sober and steadfast to his diet. He had lost thirty-five pounds and was starting to date a woman whose husband had recently died. Ned and Juanita enjoyed the Colorado mountains, spending several weekends camping in Salida, Steamboat, and Glenwood Springs.

Ned and Juanita's relationship would only last a few months. Ned Kranepool was killed by a drunk driver who was speeding at one hundred ten miles per hour on I70, despite a heavy snowstorm.

. . .

JUANITA SANGUILLEN had to bury another man who she loved. However, she mourned Ned Kranepool differently than Hank Sanguillen.

Juanita was keeping a deep, dark secret. She was a murderer.

In the wee hours of the morning following another Game Night that Juanita and Hank would not attend, Hank woke Juanita to tell her he was taking Mongo for a walk. It had been a rough day for the couple. Hank had been terminated for failing to show up for work, his fifth unexcused absence. Turned out Hank Sanguillen would skip work and follow Linda O'Neill to her job, stalking the woman who was more addicting to him than heroin. Linda had long since ended things with Hank, and Hank had married Juanita, but Hank simply could not shake the fixation on Linda O'Neill.

Hank did not take his cell phone on the dog walk. Juanita knew his phone password. She had her suspicions. Those weird calls from Kerri-Anne raised many concerns. And Hank always had his phone in his hand, except for that one fateful night. Mongo had awakened Hank from a deep sleep, and Hank was too tired to realize he had forgotten the phone.

Juanita had to peek. What she saw boiled her insides. Thousands of texts to Linda, although she would rarely reply, except to ask about Game Night. There were photos of Linda as well—creepy, stalker photos of Linda undressing, apparently taken from outside Linda's home.

Juanita was in love with Hank Sanguillen. The high from their wonderful honeymoon crashed down into a deep chasm of instant depression. Juanita went to the backyard and grabbed the pole from the wrought-iron fence that Mongo had knocked loose. When Hank and

Mongo returned, Juanita confronted him in their driveway.

"I know everything, you bastard."

"Know what?"

"You and Linda. How dare you? We were *just* married. She doesn't want you, anyway. Can't you see that?"

Hank stood motionless and speechless, Mongo tugging to go back inside.

Juanita blocked Hank's path to the house, continuing to admonish her husband. "What does that woman have that I don't?"

Hank finally spoke: "I can't explain it, hon. She just has ... something."

"You don't get to call me 'hon' anymore." Juanita swung the long metal pole out from behind her back and jabbed it into Hank's midsection. Hank collapsed immediately to the cement driveway.

Hank was a big man, so it was difficult for Juanita to hoist his dead body into her SUV. She used a refrigerator dolly to assist. And then Juanita drove her deceased husband to the Platte River, where she deposited his corpse. But the river flow carried Hank to shore, where coyotes and birds of prey would savage his body. Then Juanita returned home and power-washed the driveway clean from Hank's blood. She fully expected the police to suspect her and prepared herself for the possibility of life behind bars. But that never happened.

Even when Ren DeJesus was fleeing the police, Juanita watched the events unfold from her window, clutching onto the long metal pole that was Hank Sanguillen's murder weapon, a wry little smile affixed to her face.

Ren DeJesus sat in a prison cell for a crime he did not commit. Yet no one ever searched Juanita's home for a long sharp object. No one suspected Juanita Sanguillen in the death of her husband. Ned Kranepool never found out Juanita killed Hank. No one ever found out.

Juanita did not try to plan the perfect murder. It simply turned out that way.

THE END

ABOUT THE AUTHOR

Ted Huntington peaked as an writer at age eight... and he has been working to regain that fame ever since.

Seriously, second grade Ted wrote a play called "Blast Off to Ecaps" that was performed by his class. Fast-forward some 35 years, and Ted turned the play into the young adult novel of the same title, following it up two years later with "Blast Off to Earth."

A writing "addict," Ted has always used his writing talents throughout his career, which has taken him to successful stints as a marketing and advertising executive.

Now primarily focused on writing, Ted has authored "Doug Maxwell," a supernatural/superhero novel, a poetry anthology, "Uplifting: Poems of Positivity," and he is working on additional novels and screenplays.

To learn more about Theodore Huntington and discover more Next Chapter authors, visit our website at www.nextchapter.pub.

The Game Night Murders
ISBN: 978-4-82416-817-7
Mass Market

Published by
Next Chapter
2-5-6 SANNO
SANNO BRIDGE
143-0023 Ota-Ku, Tokyo
+818035793528

7th February 2023

9 784824 168177